GLUSKABE

AND THE

FOUR WISHES

RETOLD BY

Joseph Bruchac

ILLUSTRATED BY

Christine Nyburg Shrader

COBBLEHILL BOOKS/Dutton · New York

For Doris Minkler and Cecile Wawanolet,
Abenaki elders who teach the best wishes are unselfish ones
Ktsi oleohneh! (Great thanks!)

JB

To my buddy Stephen,
with special artist-thanks to Lee Blodget and Cherry Brown.

CNS

Library of Congress Cataloging-in-Publication Data
Bruchac, Joseph, date.
Gluskabe and the four wishes / retold by Joseph Bruchac ;
illustrated by Christine Shrader.
p.   cm.
Summary: Four Abenaki men set out on a difficult journey to
ask the great hero Gluskabe to grant each his fondest wish.
ISBN 0-525-65164-0
1. Abnaki Indians—Legends.   [1. Abnaki Indians—Legends.
2. Indians of North America—Legends.]   I. Shrader, Christine, ill.   II. Title.
E99.A13B78   1995   398.2′089973—dc20   93-26924   CIP   AC
Published in the United States by Cobblehill Books,
an affiliate of Dutton Children's Books,
a division of Penguin Books USA Inc.,
375 Hudson Street, New York, New York 10014
Designed by Kathleen Westray
Printed in Hong Kong
First edition   10 9 8 7 6 5 4 3 2 1

AUTHOR'S NOTE

Gluskabe and the Four Wishes is a traditional story told in various ways among the Wabanaki peoples of New England. (Wabanaki includes the Abenaki-language-speaking Native Nations of the Micmac, Malisett, Penobscot, Passamaquoddy, and Western Abenaki. My own tribal registration is with the Western Abenaki Nation in Swanton, Vermont.)

Because of the Indian ancestry in my family, I have spent much of my adult life seeking out traditional stories and listening to the way they are still told by Native elders in many parts of the continent. As I did with this story, I usually research all of the written versions of any tale (there are at least four different written versions of this story), compare those written versions with oral tellings I have heard, and then craft my own telling of the story.

These stories are strong teaching stories, ones which are meant to be entertaining so that they will carry their lessons that much more effectively.

Gluskabe is a culture hero of the Western Abenaki peoples, including the Penobscot Indians. Among the nations farther to the east, such as the Passamaquoddy and Micmac, the spelling of his name is Koluskap or Glooskap. He and his wise grandmother, Woodchuck, were here on earth before the human beings came and Gluskabe has often served as a helper to *Ktsi Nwaskw,* the Great Spirit, the Creator of all things. Petonbowk is a western Abenaki word meaning "waters in between," the name for Lake Champlain.

JOSEPH BRUCHAC

LONG AGO, Gluskabe lived with his grandmother, Woodchuck, near the big water. Gluskabe is the one who defeated the monster which tried to keep all the water in the world for himself. He is the one who made the big animals grow small so they would be less dangerous to human beings.

When Gluskabe had done many things to make the world a better place for his children and his children's children, he decided it was time to rest. He went down to the big water, climbed into his magic canoe made of stone, and sailed away to a far island. Some say that island is in the great lake the people call Petonbowk. Others say they went far to the east, beyond the coast of Maine.

They say the fog which rises out there is actually the smoke
from Gluskabe's pipe. It is said that for a time Gluskabe let it be
known to the world that anyone who came to him would be granted
one wish.

Once there were four Abenaki men who decided to make the
journey to visit Gluskabe.

One of them was a man who had almost no possessions. His wish was that Gluskabe would make it so that he owned many fine things.

The second man was very vain. He was already quite tall, but he wore his hair piled up high on his head and stuffed moss into his moccasins so that he would be even greater in height. He wished to be taller than all men.

The third man was very afraid of dying. His wish was that he would live longer than any man.

The fourth man spent much time hunting to provide food for his family and village. But he was not a very good hunter, even though he tried very hard. His wish was that he would become a good enough hunter to always give his people enough to eat.

The four of them set out in a canoe to find Gluskabe. Their trip was not an easy one. The currents were very strong and they had to paddle hard against them. The man who owned nothing knew a song to calm the waters and when he sang it the currents ceased and they were able to go on their way.

Now a wind began to blow very hard, pushing them back toward shore. The second man offered tobacco to the wind and it became calm enough for them to continue.

Soon great whales began to come near the canoe and it seemed as if they would tip the boat over. But the man who was afraid of dying had brought with him a small stone figure shaped like a whale. He dropped it into the water and the whales dove beneath the surface and were gone.

Now the island of Gluskabe was very close, but they could not see it because a fog came over the water and hid everything. The fourth man, who wanted to be a good hunter, took out his pipe and began to smoke it, asking Gluskabe to stop smoking his own pipe and let the fog lift. Soon the fog rolled away and they saw the island of Gluskabe before them.

They left their canoe on the shore and made their way to the place where Gluskabe sat. *"Kuai!"* Gluskabe said. "You have had to work hard to come here to see me. You have each earned the right to make one wish."

"I wish to own many fine possessions," said the first man.

"My wish is to be taller than any man," said the second.

"I want to live longer than any man," said the third.

"My desire is not so much for myself," said the fourth man. "I want to be a good enough hunter to provide food for my family and my people."

Gluskabe looked at the fourth man and smiled. Then he took out four pouches and gave one to each of the men.

"In each of these you will find what you want. But do not open them before you get home and in your own lodges."

The men all agreed and went back to the canoe. They crossed the waters and reached the land. Then each of them started on his own way home.

The first man, who wanted many possessions, was given the canoe which had belonged to the one who wanted to live longer than any man.

"Take this to go home in," he said. "I am going to live forever, so it will be easy for me to make another canoe."

As the man who wanted many possessions paddled along he thought about all that he would have. He would have fine clothing of buckskin, he would have ornaments made of shells and bright beads, he would have stone axes and finely made weapons, he would have a beautiful lodge to live in. As he thought about all the things he would have he grew more and more anxious to see them.

Finally he could wait no longer.

"It will not hurt anything if I just peek inside this pouch," he said. He opened it just a crack to look inside.

As soon as he did so all kinds of things began to pour out of the pouch. Moccasins and shirts, necklaces and wampum belts, axes and spears, and bows and arrows. The man tried to close the pouch but he could not do so. The things came pouring out and filled the canoe, covering the man. They were so heavy that the canoe sank and the man, tangled in all his possessions, sank with them.

The second man, who wanted to be taller than all others, had walked along for only a short time before he, too, became curious. He stopped on top of a high ridge and took out the pouch.

"How can this make me taller?" he said. "Perhaps there is some kind of magic ointment in here that I can rub on myself to make me grow. There would be nothing wrong with trying just a little of it before I get home."

Then he opened the pouch.

As soon as he did so he was transformed into a pine, the tallest of the trees. To this day, the pines stand taller than all others, growing on the high ridges. In the wind you may hear them whispering, bragging about their height, taller than all men.

The third man, too, did not go far before he became curious. "If I am going to live forever," he said, "then nothing will be able to hurt me. Thus there is no reason why I should not open this pouch."

He opened it up.

As soon as he did so he turned into a great boulder, one which could stand unchanged for thousands of seasons, longer than the life of any man.

The fourth man, though, did not think of himself as he traveled home. He had farther to go than the others, but he did not stop. "Soon," he said to himself, "I will be able to feed my people." He went straight to his lodge and when he got inside he opened the pouch.

But there was nothing inside it.

Yet as he sat there, holding the open pouch, there came into his mind a great understanding. He realized the ways he must proceed to hunt animals. He began to understand how to prepare himself for a hunt and how to show the animals respect so that they would always allow him to hunt. It seemed he could hear someone speaking to him, more than one person. Then he realized he was hearing the voices of the animals themselves, telling him about their ways.

From that day on he was the best hunter among the people. He never took more game than was needed, yet he always provided enough to feed his people.

His was truly the best of the gifts given by Gluskabe.